LOST LOVE IN TOKYO

Lost Love in Tokyo

Love Stories Around the World, Volume 2

Mikey

Published by Mikey, 2024.

This is a work of fiction. Similarities to real people, places, or events are entirely coincidental.

LOST LOVE IN TOKYO

First edition. April 27, 2024.

Copyright © 2024 Mikey.

ISBN: 979-8224602490

Written by Mikey.

To all the dreamers, the romantics, and the believers in love's enduring magic—this book is for you. May its pages remind you that love knows no bounds, and that with every heartbeat, a new love story begins.

MIKEY KATODIYA

Copyright © Mikey Katodiya
All Rights Reserved.

This book has been self-published with all reasonable efforts taken to make the material error-free by the author. No part of this book shall be used, reproduced in any manner whatsoever without written permission from the author, except in the case of brief quotations embodied in critical articles and reviews.

The Author of this book is solely responsible and liable for its content including but not limited to the views, representations, descriptions, statements, information, opinions and references ["Content"]. The Content of this book shall not constitute or be construed or deemed to reflect the opinion or expression of the Publisher or Editor. Neither the Publisher nor Editor endorse or approve the Content of this book or guarantee the reliability, accuracy or completeness of the Content published herein and do not make any representations or warranties of any kind, express or implied, including but not limited to the implied warranties of merchantability, fitness for a particular purpose. The Publisher and Editor shall not be liable whatsoever for any errors, omissions, whether such errors or omissions result from negligence, accident, or any other cause or claims for loss or damages of any kind, including without limitation, indirect or consequential loss or damage arising out of use, inability to use, or about the reliability, accuracy or sufficiency of the information contained in this book.

Made with ❤ Mikey Katodiya

Foreword

Welcome to "Lost Love in Tokyo," a captivating tale that will transport you to the vibrant streets of Tokyo and immerse you in a love story that transcends time and space.

In this book, you will journey alongside Akira and Emi, two souls bound by destiny and intertwined in the intricate dance of love. Their story is not just a narrative but a melody of emotions, a symphony of longing, passion, and resilience that will resonate with your heart.

As you turn the pages, allow yourself to be swept away by the sights, sounds, and sensations of Tokyo—the bustling energy of Shibuya, the serene beauty of Ueno Park, and the hidden gems of Harajuku's alleyways. These settings are not merely backdrops but characters in their own right, shaping the narrative and adding depth to the journey of our protagonists.

But beyond the cityscape lies the beating heart of this story—Akira and Emi's love. It is a love that defies distance, conquers adversity, and blooms like a sakura tree in full bloom, its petals whispering secrets of passion and devotion.

Prepare to embark on a rollercoaster of emotions—a journey of discovery, growth, and the unyielding power of love to illuminate even the darkest corners of our souls. "Lost Love in Tokyo" is not just a story; it's an experience—an invitation to delve into the depths of human connection and the eternal quest for a love that transcends all boundaries.

So, dear reader, fasten your seatbelt, open your heart, and let the magic of "Lost Love in Tokyo" sweep you off your feet into a world where love knows no limits and dreams take flight amidst the neon lights and cherry blossoms of Tokyo's enchanting landscape.

Preface

In the heart of Tokyo, where skyscrapers kiss the sky and cherry blossoms paint the streets with delicate hues of pink, a love story unfolds—a tale as timeless as the city itself yet as fresh as the morning dew on a spring day.

"Lost Love in Tokyo" invites you to step into a world where love knows no boundaries, where passion ignites like fireworks against the night sky, and where every corner holds the promise of a new adventure.

But before we dive into the depths of this captivating narrative, let me take you on a journey behind the scenes—the genesis of Akira and Emi's story, the inspiration that breathed life into these characters, and the magic that infuses every page of this book.

As the author, I found myself drawn to Tokyo's dynamic energy, its blend of ancient tradition and modern innovation, and above all, its ability to stir the soul and awaken the senses. It was within this vibrant tapestry of sights, sounds, and emotions that Akira and Emi's love story took root and blossomed into a tale that I am honored to share with you.

Within these pages, you will encounter not just characters but kindred spirits—individuals who mirror our hopes, fears, dreams, and aspirations. Akira embodies the courage to pursue love against all odds, while Emi represents the resilience to weather life's storms with grace and strength.

Together, they navigate the complexities of relationships, the nuances of communication, and the transformative power of forgiveness. Their journey is a mirror of our own—a reflection of the universal quest for connection, understanding, and the enduring quest for a love that stands the test of time.

So, as you embark on this literary adventure, I invite you to open your heart, suspend disbelief, and allow yourself to be swept away by the magic of "Lost Love in Tokyo." May it inspire you, touch your soul, and remind you that amidst the chaos of life, love remains the beacon that guides us home.

Acknowledgements

In the tapestry of storytelling, there are countless threads that weave together to create a masterpiece. "Lost Love in Tokyo" is no exception, and I am deeply grateful for the many hands, hearts, and minds that contributed to bringing this book to life.

First and foremost, I extend my heartfelt gratitude to the city of Tokyo itself, with its pulsating energy, captivating beauty, and rich tapestry of culture. Tokyo served as both the backdrop and the muse for this story, inspiring me at every turn and infusing the narrative with its unique charm and allure.

To my characters, Akira and Emi, thank you for entrusting me with your story. Your journey of love, loss, and rediscovery has touched my heart in ways I never imagined, and I am honored to have been a part of your world.

To my readers, your enthusiasm, feedback, and unwavering support have been a constant source of motivation and inspiration. Your love for storytelling fuels my passion and drives me to create narratives that resonate with your hearts and minds.

I extend my gratitude to my family and friends for their endless encouragement, understanding, and belief in my creative endeavors. Your love and support have been the foundation upon which I built this book, and I am eternally grateful for your presence in my life.

To my editors, beta readers, and publishing team, thank you for your expertise, guidance, and dedication to crafting a polished and compelling narrative. Your insights and feedback have been invaluable in shaping "Lost Love in Tokyo" into the book it is today.

Last but certainly not least, I express my deepest gratitude to the readers who have embarked on this literary journey with me. Your curiosity, imagination, and passion for storytelling are the driving force behind every word I write.

Together, we have woven a tale of love, resilience, and the enduring power of connection—a tapestry that I hope will continue to inspire, uplift, and bring joy to all who encounter it.

With heartfelt thanks and warm wishes,
Mikey Katodiya

Prologue

In the heart of Tokyo, where the city's pulse beats with a rhythm all its own, there exists a hidden world—a world where dreams and reality intertwine, where love and longing dance in the moonlit shadows, and where every street corner holds a story waiting to be told.

Our journey begins not with a bang but with a whisper—a whisper of a love lost, a whisper of a love found, and a whisper of a love that defies the boundaries of time and space.

Meet Akira, a young artist with a heart as vibrant as the city he calls home. His brushstrokes capture the essence of Tokyo—its bustling streets, its tranquil gardens, and its hidden alleyways where secrets linger like cherry blossoms in the spring.

And then there's Emi, a free spirit whose laughter echoes through the city like a melody. Her passion for life is infectious, her curiosity boundless, and her heart yearns for a love that transcends the ordinary.

Their paths cross one fateful night, amid the neon glow of Shibuya and the whispers of the wind in Yoyogi Park. It is a meeting that sparks a fire—a fire of attraction, of connection, and of a love that ignites like a shooting star across the Tokyo skyline.

But as with all great love stories, theirs is not without its challenges. Fate conspires, misunderstandings arise, and the distance between them stretches like the Sumida River at dusk. Yet, amidst the chaos and uncertainty, their love remains a beacon—a guiding light that leads them back to each other time and time again.

Join us as we embark on a journey of love, loss, and rediscovery—a journey that takes us beyond the streets of Tokyo and into the depths of the human heart. For in this city of contrasts, where tradition meets modernity and dreams collide with reality, Akira and Emi's love story unfolds—a story that reminds us that sometimes, the greatest adventures begin with a whisper.

I

A Chance Encounter in Tokyo

The bustling streets of Tokyo pulsed with life as Akira navigated through the crowd, his eyes searching for something he couldn't quite name. He had just moved to the city, hoping to start fresh after a painful breakup. As he walked past a charming café, his gaze met Emi's for the first time.

Emi, a talented artist, was sketching the cityscape when Akira's presence caught her attention. Their eyes locked briefly, a moment charged with unspoken curiosity and a hint of recognition. Akira paused, captivated by the way Emi's eyes seemed to hold a universe of stories.

In that fleeting moment, something shifted within them. It was as if fate had woven a delicate thread, connecting their souls in a way neither could explain. Akira hesitated, torn between the urge to walk away and the pull to stay and unravel the mystery that surrounded Emi.

Before he could make a decision, a sudden downpour engulfed the street, sending everyone scrambling for cover. Emi hurriedly packed her sketching materials, casting a wistful glance at Akira before disappearing into the café.

For days after that encounter, Akira found himself haunted by thoughts of Emi. He wandered the streets, hoping to catch another glimpse of her, but she remained elusive. It was as if their meeting had been a fleeting dream, leaving Akira wondering if he had imagined the connection they shared.

As weeks passed, Akira immersed himself in his work, trying to push aside the memories of Emi. Yet, her image lingered in the corners of his mind, a constant reminder of the unanswered questions that hung between them.

Little did he know, fate had more in store for them than just a chance encounter on a rainy day in Tokyo.

II

The Art of Serendipity

As the days turned into weeks, Akira's life settled into a rhythm. He threw himself into his work, finding solace in the routine of his daily activities. Yet, despite his efforts to move on, Emi's image continued to linger in his thoughts, a constant presence that tugged at his heart.

One evening, while walking home from work, Akira stumbled upon an art exhibition showcasing local talents. Intrigued, he stepped inside, his eyes scanning the vibrant paintings and intricate sculptures. And there, amidst the sea of art, he spotted Emi's name on a plaque next to a captivating piece.

It was as if destiny had orchestrated their reunion, bringing them together once again in a space filled with creativity and possibility. Akira couldn't tear his gaze away from Emi's artwork, each stroke of her brush revealing a glimpse of her soul.

Lost in the beauty of her creations, Akira didn't notice Emi approaching until she stood beside him, a smile playing on her lips. Their eyes met, and for a moment, the world around them faded into insignificance. It was as if time had stood still, allowing them to savor the magic of their reunion.

Emi's voice broke the silence, her words tentative yet filled with warmth. She spoke of her journey as an artist, sharing snippets of her life that mirrored Akira's own experiences. In that shared moment, they discovered a connection that went beyond words—a bond forged through shared dreams and aspirations.

As they talked, Akira couldn't shake off the feeling that their paths were meant to cross once again. It was a realization that filled him with both excitement and trepidation, knowing that their reunion could either lead to new beginnings or reopen old wounds.

But as they laughed and reminisced about their chance encounter in the rain, Akira felt a sense of hope blooming within him. Perhaps, amidst the chaos of life, serendipity had a way of bringing two lost souls together, weaving their stories into a tapestry of love and possibility.

III

Echoes of the Past

The days that followed Emi and Akira's reunion at the art exhibition were filled with a delicate dance of hesitation and longing. They exchanged occasional messages, each word carrying the weight of unspoken emotions and unanswered questions.

One evening, as Tokyo's skyline was painted in hues of twilight, Akira found himself standing outside the café where he had first seen Emi. The memories of their initial encounter flooded his mind, stirring a whirlwind of emotions within him.

As if on cue, Emi appeared at the café's entrance, a hesitant smile on her lips. Their eyes met, and for a moment, time seemed to stand still. It was a moment of recognition and vulnerability, as if they were both silently acknowledging the bond that had formed between them.

They sat at a corner table, sipping steaming cups of tea as they delved into conversations that meandered through past experiences and shared dreams. Emi spoke of her love for art and the stories hidden within her paintings, while Akira shared snippets of his journey to Tokyo and the longing that had brought him to this moment.

As the night deepened, their conversation turned introspective, exploring the complexities of love and loss. Emi spoke of a past love that had shaped her art, while Akira opened up about the pain of a failed relationship that still lingered in his heart.

In that intimate exchange of stories, they found solace in each other's vulnerabilities. It was a cathartic experience, weaving together the threads of their pasts into a tapestry of understanding and empathy.

As they bid farewell that night, a sense of anticipation hung in the air—a silent agreement to explore the uncharted territory of their budding connection. For Emi and Akira, the echoes of the past were not just memories but stepping stones toward a future filled with possibilities.

IV

Whispers of Love

In the days that followed their heartfelt conversation at the café, Emi and Akira found themselves drawn to each other like magnets, their bond growing stronger with each passing moment.

One afternoon, Akira surprised Emi with a visit to her art studio. The space was a reflection of her creativity, filled with canvases that told stories of love, loss, and resilience. Emi's eyes lit up as she showed Akira around, sharing the inspiration behind each painting.

As they stood amidst colors and brushstrokes, a sense of intimacy enveloped them. Akira couldn't help but marvel at Emi's talent and the emotions she poured into her art. It was a glimpse into her soul, a testament to her ability to capture the essence of human emotions on canvas.

Emi, in turn, was captivated by Akira's presence, his quiet strength and unwavering support. They spent hours talking about their dreams and aspirations, each revelation deepening their connection.

As the sun set outside, casting a warm glow over the studio, Akira took Emi's hand in his, a silent promise of solidarity and affection. In that moment, words were unnecessary as their hearts spoke a language of love that transcended the confines of speech.

Days turned into weeks, and their bond blossomed into a tender romance filled with stolen glances and shared laughter. They explored Tokyo together, discovering hidden gems in the city's labyrinthine streets and creating memories that would last a lifetime.

But amidst the joy of newfound love, whispers of doubt crept into Akira's mind. He couldn't shake off the fear of repeating past mistakes, of losing something precious once again. As he gazed into Emi's eyes, he knew he had to confront his fears and lay bare his heart, for their love deserved nothing less than honesty and vulnerability.

V

Tides of Vulnerability

As Akira grappled with his inner turmoil, Emi sensed a shift in his demeanor. The once carefree moments they shared now carried a tinge of hesitation, leaving her heart heavy with unspoken worries.

One evening, as they sat by the riverbank watching the city lights dance on the water's surface, Emi gently broached the subject that had been weighing on her mind. She spoke of her fears and uncertainties, laying bare her vulnerabilities in front of Akira.

Her words hung in the air, mingling with the soft breeze that rustled through the trees. Akira listened intently, his own fears mirrored in Emi's honest confession. He spoke of his past heartbreaks and the walls he had built around his heart to protect himself from pain.

In that moment of shared vulnerability, a bridge of understanding formed between them. They realized that love was not just about basking in the joys of companionship but also about navigating the storms of doubt and fear together.

With a newfound resolve, Akira opened his heart to Emi, expressing his love and devotion in words that echoed across the river. Emi, touched by his honesty, embraced him tightly, feeling the weight of their unspoken fears lift from their shoulders.

From that day onward, their relationship blossomed into a haven of trust and acceptance. They learned to communicate openly, to share their hopes and dreams without fear of judgment or rejection.

As they walked hand in hand through Tokyo's bustling streets, their love shone like a beacon of hope, a testament to the resilience of the human heart. For Emi and Akira, the tides of vulnerability had not drowned their love but had strengthened it, forging a bond that was unbreakable.

VI

Laughter in the Rain

As Emi and Akira's love deepened, they found joy in the simple moments they shared together. One rainy afternoon, as they took shelter under a shared umbrella, a playful banter ensued, punctuated by laughter that echoed in the pitter-patter of raindrops.

Akira, with a mischievous twinkle in his eyes, challenged Emi to a race through the rain-soaked streets. Emi, never one to back down from a challenge, accepted with a grin, her laughter mingling with the rhythm of their footsteps.

They raced through puddles and dodged umbrellas, their carefree antics drawing smiles from passersby. In that moment of childlike spontaneity, they forgot their worries and embraced the simple joy of being alive.

As they reached the end of their impromptu race, breathless and exhilarated, Akira pulled Emi into a warm embrace, raindrops mingling with tears of laughter on their cheeks. It was a moment of pure happiness, a snapshot of their love story painted in shades of laughter and rain.

But amidst the laughter, a sense of gratitude washed over them—a reminder of the preciousness of each moment they shared together. They stood in the rain, hearts full and spirits renewed, ready to face whatever challenges life threw their way with laughter as their armor and love as their guide.

VII

Whispers of Longing

As the seasons changed and Tokyo embraced the colors of autumn, Emi and Akira found themselves caught in the bittersweet symphony of longing and love.

One evening, as they strolled through a park adorned with golden leaves, a sense of nostalgia swept over them. Emi paused to sketch the vibrant hues of nature, her fingers tracing the lines of memories that intertwined with each stroke of her pencil.

Akira watched her with a tender smile, his heart brimming with admiration for her talent and the emotions she infused into her art. He knew that behind every stroke lay a story—a tale of love, loss, and the unspoken yearning that echoed in the whispers of autumn leaves.

As dusk descended and the park grew quiet, Emi shared a secret with Akira—a dream she had long harbored but never dared to voice aloud. She spoke of a desire to travel beyond Tokyo, to explore distant lands and immerse herself in different cultures.

Her words stirred something within Akira—a mix of pride for her ambitions and a pang of longing at the thought of being apart. Yet, he knew that love meant supporting each other's dreams, even if it meant facing the ache of separation.

With a bittersweet smile, Akira vowed to stand by Emi's side, encouraging her to chase her dreams while holding onto the promise of their love that transcended distance and time.

And so, amidst the whispers of longing carried by the autumn breeze, Emi and Akira made plans for a future filled with adventures, knowing that no matter where life took them, their love would always be the anchor that kept them grounded.

VIII

Dreams Across Borders

Emi's dream of traveling beyond Tokyo ignited a spark of excitement in both her and Akira. They spent evenings planning their adventures, poring over maps and guidebooks, dreaming of the places they would explore together.

As the days grew shorter and winter descended upon Tokyo, Emi received an opportunity to showcase her artwork in an international exhibition. It was a chance to fulfill her dream of traveling abroad and sharing her passion for art with a global audience.

Akira, filled with pride and a hint of sadness at the thought of being apart, encouraged Emi to seize the opportunity. He promised to support her from afar, cheering her on as she embarked on this new chapter of her artistic journey.

With a mix of excitement and apprehension, Emi boarded a plane bound for Paris, the city of love and art. As she walked the cobblestone streets, her heart fluttered with anticipation, her thoughts filled with Akira and the love that bridged the distance between them.

Meanwhile, back in Tokyo, Akira immersed himself in his work, finding solace in the memories of their shared moments and the promise of a reunion that awaited them.

Across borders and time zones, Emi and Akira stayed connected through letters filled with words of love and encouragement. They shared snippets of their experiences, from Emi's enchantment with Parisian cafes to Akira's discoveries in Tokyo's hidden alleyways.

Despite the physical distance, their love grew stronger, fueled by the shared dreams they nurtured together. And as spring bloomed in Tokyo, Emi returned home, her heart brimming with stories of adventure and a renewed appreciation for the love that had guided her across borders and back into Akira's arms.

IX

Blossoms of Reunion

Spring arrived in Tokyo with a burst of cherry blossoms, painting the city in hues of pink and white. Emi's return from Paris was a celebration of love and reunion, as Akira eagerly awaited her arrival at the airport.

As Emi stepped off the plane, her eyes met Akira's, and time seemed to stand still. In that moment, amidst the bustling airport crowd, they found each other again, their love radiating like the blooming sakura trees.

Akira greeted Emi with a bouquet of cherry blossoms, a symbol of their enduring love and the beauty of new beginnings. They walked hand in hand through the streets adorned with petals, sharing stories of their time apart and the moments that had shaped them.

Emi's experiences in Paris had enriched her artistry, infusing her paintings with a new depth and perspective. She unveiled her latest masterpiece—a canvas that captured the essence of their love, intertwined with the beauty of cherry blossoms and the whispers of distant lands.

For Akira, seeing Emi's growth and creativity blossom filled his heart with pride and admiration. He knew that their love story was not just about the moments they shared but also about the individual journeys that shaped them into who they were.

As they sat beneath a canopy of cherry blossoms, their laughter mingling with the soft rustle of petals, Emi and Akira reveled in the beauty of their reunion. It was a moment of gratitude and joy, a testament to the resilience of love that had weathered storms and bloomed like the sakura—a symbol of hope, renewal, and endless possibilities.

X

Harmony of Hearts

As the days lengthened and summer embraced Tokyo in its warm embrace, Emi and Akira found themselves immersed in a harmonious rhythm of love and creativity.

They spent lazy afternoons in Emi's art studio, where the sunlight streamed through the windows, casting a golden glow on their shared moments of inspiration. Akira became Emi's muse, his presence igniting a spark of creativity that danced across her canvases.

Together, they explored new mediums of art, experimenting with colors and textures that mirrored the vibrancy of their love. Emi's paintings became a reflection of their journey—a tapestry of emotions woven with strokes of passion and tenderness.

One evening, as they sat on the balcony overlooking Tokyo's skyline, Emi unveiled her latest creation—a collaborative piece that captured the essence of their love story. It was a fusion of their artistic styles, a symphony of colors and lines that spoke of unity and harmony.

Akira marveled at the masterpiece before him, seeing their love mirrored in every brushstroke. He knew that their bond went beyond words, transcending the boundaries of art and reality.

As they embraced under the starlit sky, surrounded by the sounds of the city coming to life, Emi and Akira knew that their love was a melody that resonated in the hearts of those who witnessed it. It was a harmony of souls, a symphony of love that would continue to crescendo with each passing day, creating a masterpiece of their own making.

XI

Whispers of Change

As summer faded into the gentle embrace of autumn, Emi and Akira felt a subtle shift in the air—a whisper of change that stirred their hearts with both anticipation and apprehension.

They sat together in their favorite café, sipping steaming cups of tea as they watched the leaves outside dance to the rhythm of the wind. Emi's gaze was distant, her thoughts drifting to the dreams she had yet to chase, while Akira's eyes held a silent question, a yearning for clarity in the midst of uncertainty.

In the quiet moments between conversations, they sensed the unspoken longing for growth and exploration. Emi spoke of her desire to travel once again, to immerse herself in new cultures and draw inspiration from the world beyond Tokyo's borders.

Akira listened, his heart torn between the comfort of familiarity and the allure of adventure. He knew that change was inevitable, that life was a series of chapters waiting to be written. Yet, the thought of stepping into the unknown filled him with a mixture of excitement and trepidation.

They walked through the city streets, hand in hand, lost in their thoughts yet connected by an invisible thread of love. The autumn leaves whispered secrets of transformation, of letting go of old patterns to make room for new beginnings.

As they stood by the riverbank, watching the sun set in a blaze of colors, Emi turned to Akira with determination in her eyes. She spoke of their shared dreams, of the possibilities that awaited them beyond the familiar horizon.

Akira nodded, his heart echoing her words. He knew that change would bring challenges, but it would also open doors to new experiences and growth. Together, they embraced the whispers of change, ready to embark on a journey of discovery and transformation, knowing that their love would be the constant guiding light in the ever-changing landscape of their lives.

XII

Embracing New Horizons

The whispers of change lingered in the air as Emi and Akira stood on the cusp of new horizons. They spent nights discussing their dreams, weaving plans for the future that intertwined their individual aspirations with the shared vision of a life filled with love and adventure.

Emi's passion for art and travel had ignited a fire within her, propelling her to explore new artistic mediums and immerse herself in diverse cultures. Akira, inspired by her determination, found himself embracing change with a newfound sense of purpose.

One morning, as Tokyo woke to the first hints of winter, Emi received an invitation to participate in an artist residency program in Barcelona—a chance to collaborate with artists from around the world and showcase her work on an international stage.

The news filled Emi with excitement and a touch of nervousness, knowing that the journey ahead would be filled with challenges and opportunities for growth. Akira, sensing her mixed emotions, stood by her side, offering unwavering support and encouragement.

They spent days packing and preparing for Emi's trip, their home buzzing with anticipation and a sense of adventure. As they stood at the airport, saying their farewells amidst tearful goodbyes and promises of reunion, Emi and Akira knew that distance would only strengthen their bond.

Barcelona welcomed Emi with open arms, its vibrant culture and artistic energy fueling her creativity. She immersed herself in the residency program, collaborating with fellow artists and drawing inspiration from the city's rich history and architectural marvels.

Meanwhile, back in Tokyo, Akira continued to pursue his own passions, finding solace in the memories of their time together and the anticipation of Emi's return.

Across continents and time zones, their love remained steadfast, bridging the physical distance with heartfelt letters, late-night calls, and dreams of reunion under the starlit sky. For Emi and Akira, embracing new horizons was not just about geographical exploration but also about the journey of self-discovery and the unbreakable bond that held them together, no matter where life took them.

XIII

Echoes of Absence

As Emi immersed herself in the artistic vibrancy of Barcelona, Akira navigated Tokyo's familiar streets with a sense of longing that echoed in the spaces she once occupied. The absence of her laughter and presence left a void in his heart, a reminder of the bittersweet nature of love across distances.

Nights stretched into days, each moment marked by the quiet echoes of their separation. Akira filled his days with work, finding solace in routine yet yearning for the shared moments that colored his memories.

Emi, too, felt the weight of absence, the distance amplifying the whispers of doubt and longing. She poured her emotions into her art, channeling the echoes of their love story onto canvases that spoke of yearning and resilience.

Their communication became a lifeline—a symphony of words that bridged the miles between them. They shared snippets of their days, weaving tales of mundane encounters and fleeting moments of beauty that reminded them of each other.

One evening, as Akira stood on their balcony overlooking Tokyo's skyline, a gentle breeze carried with it a melody of memories. He closed his eyes, imagining Emi's laughter dancing in the wind, her presence a whisper in the starlit night.

Emi, in Barcelona, found solace in the city's artistic energy, yet a part of her heart remained tethered to Tokyo. She wandered through galleries and streets lined with graffiti, seeking traces of Akira in the vibrant tapestry of colors and emotions.

Despite the physical distance, their love remained a constant presence—an echo that reverberated in their hearts, reminding them of the deep connection that transcended time and space.

And as the days passed, the echoes of absence only served to strengthen their resolve, fueling their anticipation of the day when they would reunite and create new echoes of love that resonated across continents and lifetimes.

XIV

The Symphony of Reunion

After months of separation filled with echoes of absence, Emi and Akira's long-awaited reunion finally arrived. Barcelona's streets were adorned with festive lights, mirroring the joy that filled Emi's heart as she prepared to return to Tokyo.

Akira stood at the airport gate, his heart racing with anticipation as he waited for Emi's plane to land. The moment he caught sight of her, stepping into the bustling terminal with a smile that lit up her face, time seemed to stand still.

Their embrace was a symphony of emotions—a crescendo of longing, relief, and overwhelming love. It was as if the echoes of their separation had melted away, leaving only the melody of their reunited hearts.

As they walked hand in hand through Tokyo's familiar streets, Emi and Akira savored the simple pleasures of togetherness. They revisited their favorite spots, sharing stories of their time apart and the moments that had shaped them.

One evening, under a blanket of stars, they sat on the balcony of their home, watching the city's lights twinkle in the distance. Emi spoke of her experiences in Barcelona, the friendships forged, and the artistic inspiration she had found in the city's vibrant energy.

Akira listened, his gaze filled with admiration and love. He shared his own journey of self-discovery during their time apart, acknowledging the growth and resilience that had blossomed in their hearts.

Their reunion was not just a celebration of love but also a reaffirmation of the bond that had weathered storms and crossed continents. It was a testament to the power of love's symphony—a melody that harmonized their past, present, and future into a timeless song of togetherness.

As they leaned into each other's embrace, the echoes of absence were replaced by the sweet melody of reunion—a symphony of hearts beating in perfect harmony, creating a love story that resonated with the beauty of shared experiences and unwavering devotion.

XV

Whispers of Forever

In the aftermath of their reunion, Emi and Akira found themselves immersed in the blissful rhythm of everyday life, their love stronger than ever as they embraced the beauty of shared moments and cherished memories.

They spent weekends exploring Tokyo's hidden gems, discovering new cafes and parks that became the backdrop of their love story. With each laughter-filled outing and tender moment shared, their bond deepened, weaving a tapestry of love that spoke of eternity.

One evening, as they watched the sunset from their favorite spot by the river, Akira turned to Emi with a glint of excitement in his eyes. He spoke of his dream—a vision of a future filled with adventures, laughter, and a home that echoed with the whispers of their love.

Emi's heart swelled with happiness as she listened to Akira's words, knowing that their dreams were intertwined, their paths merging into a journey of love and companionship. She spoke of her own dreams, of creating art that inspired others and traveling the world with Akira by her side.

Their conversations flowed like a river, carrying with them the hopes and dreams that painted their future in vibrant colors. They made plans, both practical and whimsical, weaving threads of commitment and passion into the fabric of their shared life.

As they walked hand in hand under the starlit sky, Emi and Akira knew that their love was a whisper of forever—a promise to stand by each other's side, to weather life's storms together, and to celebrate every moment as a testament to the beauty of their love story.

And so, amidst the whispers of Tokyo's night, Emi and Akira embraced the future with open hearts, knowing that their love would continue to echo through time, weaving its melody into the fabric of their lives, forever entwined in the symphony of their hearts.

XVI

The Dance of Forever

Emi and Akira's love story continued to unfold like a dance, each step a graceful movement in the symphony of their lives. They embraced the ebb and flow of life's rhythms, finding joy in the shared moments and strength in their unbreakable bond.

One sunny afternoon, as they wandered through a garden adorned with blooming flowers, Akira took Emi's hand and led her into a spontaneous dance. Their laughter echoed amidst the petals, their movements a reflection of the effortless harmony they shared.

As they twirled and spun, Akira whispered words of love and devotion, his eyes reflecting the depth of his feelings. Emi's heart soared with happiness, her love for him blooming like the flowers around them.

Their dance symbolized the beauty of their relationship—a delicate balance of passion, trust, and companionship. With each step, they reaffirmed their commitment to cherish and support each other through life's joys and challenges.

As the sun began to set, casting a golden glow over the garden, Emi and Akira embraced in a tender hug, their hearts entwined in the dance of forever. They knew that their love was a timeless melody, a dance that would continue to evolve and grow with each passing day.

And so, under the canvas of the evening sky, Emi and Akira made a silent vow to keep dancing through life hand in hand, knowing that their love would always be the music that guided their steps and the dance of forever that united their souls.

XVII

Whispers of Time

As Emi and Akira continued their dance of love, they became keenly aware of the whispers of time weaving through their lives. Each moment became precious, a treasure to be savored and cherished in the tapestry of their shared journey.

One evening, as they sat under the stars in a quiet park, Akira spoke of his reflections on time—the fleeting nature of moments that once seemed infinite and the importance of living in the present. Emi nodded in understanding, her gaze filled with gratitude for the time they had shared and the moments yet to come.

They talked about their dreams for the future, acknowledging that time was both a friend and a gentle reminder of life's transient beauty. Emi expressed her desire to capture the essence of time in her art, to immortalize fleeting moments in brushstrokes that spoke of love and nostalgia.

Akira, inspired by her vision, shared his own perspective on time—the way it shaped their love story, creating a narrative of growth, resilience, and unwavering devotion. He spoke of the moments they had shared, from laughter-filled adventures to quiet nights of introspection, each one etched in their hearts forever.

As they walked hand in hand through the park, bathed in the soft glow of moonlight, Emi and Akira felt a sense of peace and contentment. Time seemed to slow down, allowing them to savor the beauty of the present moment and the love that bound them together.

And so, amidst the whispers of time, Emi and Akira embraced the journey ahead with open hearts, knowing that their love would continue to bloom and evolve, transcending the boundaries of time itself. For them, every moment was a precious gift—a whisper of eternity in the symphony of their love.

XVIII

Seasons of Love

Emi and Akira's love story unfolded like the changing seasons, each phase marked by its own beauty and significance. They embraced the cycles of life, finding joy in the rhythm of nature's transitions and the constancy of their love.

As spring bloomed once again in Tokyo, Emi and Akira found themselves drawn to the cherry blossom trees, their delicate petals a symbol of renewal and new beginnings. They walked hand in hand under the blossoms, their love mirrored in the fleeting beauty of the sakura.

Summer brought with it warm days and endless possibilities. Emi and Akira explored Tokyo's vibrant neighborhoods, discovering hidden cafes and parks that became their sanctuaries of love and laughter.

Autumn painted the city in hues of gold and amber, a reminder of the beauty of change. Emi's artistry flourished, capturing the essence of the changing seasons in her paintings, each stroke a reflection of the emotions that colored their love story.

Winter arrived with a blanket of snow, enveloping Tokyo in a quiet serenity. Emi and Akira cozied up by the fireplace, sharing stories and dreams for the future as they watched the snowflakes dance outside their window.

Through each season, their love grew deeper, rooted in the shared experiences and moments that shaped their journey. They embraced the highs and lows, knowing that love was not just about the sunny days but also about weathering the storms together.

As Tokyo transitioned from one season to the next, Emi and Akira's love remained a constant—a beacon of warmth and stability in a world of change. They understood that like the seasons, their love would continue to evolve, blossoming anew with each passing year.

And so, as they welcomed another spring together, Emi and Akira embraced the beauty of the seasons and the timeless nature of their love—a love story that transcended time, echoing through the seasons of their hearts.

XIX

Dreams That Bind

As Emi and Akira continued to traverse the seasons of their love, their dreams intertwined like threads in a tapestry, weaving a story of shared aspirations and mutual support.

One summer evening, as they watched the sunset from a hilltop overlooking Tokyo, Emi shared her dreams of establishing an art studio that would serve as a haven for aspiring artists. Akira listened intently, his eyes shining with pride and admiration for her passion and vision.

He spoke of his own dreams—a desire to start a community initiative that would bring together people from diverse backgrounds, fostering creativity and collaboration. Emi's support and encouragement fueled his determination to turn his dreams into reality.

Together, they brainstormed ideas and made plans, each step bringing them closer to the fulfillment of their shared dreams. They attended workshops, connected with like-minded individuals, and poured their hearts into creating a future that reflected their values and aspirations.

As autumn painted Tokyo in vibrant colors, Emi and Akira's dreams took shape. Emi found a quaint space for her art studio, filling it with canvases, paints, and a warm atmosphere that welcomed artists of all ages and backgrounds.

Akira launched his community initiative, organizing events and workshops that brought people together to collaborate, share ideas, and inspire positive change. The support of the community fueled his passion and determination to make a difference.

Their dreams became a source of strength and unity, binding them together in a shared purpose that went beyond their individual aspirations. They celebrated each other's successes and weathered challenges with unwavering support and love.

As winter approached, Emi and Akira stood side by side, looking out at the city they loved. Their dreams had become a reality, a testament to the power of love, determination, and mutual encouragement.

And so, as they embraced the new year with hearts full of gratitude and excitement, Emi and Akira knew that their dreams would continue to evolve and grow, intertwined in the beautiful tapestry of their love story.

XX

Echoes of Legacy

As Emi and Akira's dreams took root and blossomed, they became mindful of the legacy they were creating—not just for themselves but for future generations. They found purpose in the idea of leaving behind a positive impact on the world, a legacy of love, creativity, and compassion.

One spring afternoon, as they walked through a park filled with families enjoying the cherry blossoms, Emi and Akira spoke of their desire to build a legacy that would inspire and uplift others. They envisioned a world where love and kindness were the guiding principles, where art and community thrived in harmony.

They became involved in charitable initiatives, volunteering their time and resources to support causes close to their hearts. Emi's art became a vehicle for raising awareness and funds for social causes, while Akira's community projects brought people together to make a difference in their neighborhoods.

As the seasons changed and Tokyo embraced the warmth of summer, Emi and Akira's legacy grew with each act of kindness and generosity. They mentored aspiring artists, empowered youth to pursue their passions, and fostered a sense of unity and belonging in their community.

Their love story became intertwined with their legacy, a testament to the power of love to inspire positive change. They were no longer just individuals but stewards of a legacy that echoed through the lives they touched.

As autumn painted Tokyo in shades of gold and crimson, Emi and Akira reflected on the journey that had brought them to this moment. They were grateful for the love, challenges, growth, and shared experiences that had shaped their legacy—a legacy built on the foundation of love that would continue to echo through generations to come.

And so, as they looked towards the future with hope and determination, Emi and Akira knew that their legacy was not just a reflection of their dreams but a promise to leave the world a little brighter, a little kinder, and filled with echoes of love that transcended time.

XXI

Reflections of Gratitude

As Emi and Akira reflected on their journey—the seasons of love, the dreams that bound them, and the legacy they were building—they were filled with a profound sense of gratitude for each other and the life they had created together.

One evening, as they sat by the window of their home, watching the city lights twinkle in the distance, Emi spoke softly of her gratitude for Akira's unwavering support and love. She thanked him for standing by her side through every challenge and celebration, for being her rock and her inspiration.

Akira, touched by her words, expressed his own gratitude for Emi's presence in his life. He spoke of the joy she brought, the way her laughter filled their home, and the way her love had transformed him into a better person.

Together, they reminisced about the moments that had shaped their love story—the laughter-filled adventures, the quiet evenings of reflection, and the shared dreams that had become reality. Each memory was a testament to the depth of their connection and the beauty of their journey together.

As they looked ahead to the years to come, Emi and Akira vowed to continue nurturing their love, to cherish each moment, and to never take their blessings for granted. They knew that gratitude was the foundation of their happiness, a reminder to appreciate the small miracles that made life meaningful.

In the quiet of the night, surrounded by love and gratitude, Emi and Akira held each other close, their hearts overflowing with thankfulness for the life they had built—a life filled with love, laughter, dreams, and the echoes of a legacy that would endure for generations to come.

XXII

Embracing the Unknown

Emi and Akira's journey of love and gratitude had brought them to a point of embracing the unknown with open hearts and minds. They had learned that life's greatest adventures often awaited beyond the familiar, in the uncharted territories of dreams and aspirations.

One crisp autumn morning, as they sipped tea on their balcony, Emi expressed her longing for new experiences and challenges. She spoke of her desire to travel to distant lands, to immerse herself in different cultures, and to capture the beauty of the world through her art.

Akira nodded in understanding, his own sense of curiosity piqued by Emi's words. He shared his own aspirations of exploring new avenues of creativity, of pushing boundaries and venturing into unexplored territories of his passions.

Their conversation sparked a sense of excitement and anticipation, igniting a shared dream of embarking on a journey of discovery together. They made plans to travel to Europe, to wander through cobblestone streets, visit art galleries, and soak in the rich tapestry of history and culture.

As they packed their bags and prepared for their adventure, Emi and Akira felt a sense of liberation and exhilaration. They were stepping into the unknown with a sense of wonder and curiosity, ready to embrace the surprises and joys that awaited them.

Their journey was not just about exploring new places but also about deepening their bond, experiencing life's wonders together, and creating memories that would last a lifetime.

And so, as they boarded the plane bound for Europe, Emi and Akira held hands, their hearts filled with excitement for the adventures that lay ahead. They were ready to embrace the unknown, knowing that with love as their compass, every step of the journey would be a cherished moment in the tapestry of their love story.

XXIII

Wanderlust and Wonder

Emi and Akira's journey across Europe was a tapestry woven with moments of wanderlust and wonder. From the charming streets of Paris to the historic sites of Rome, they immersed themselves in the beauty and diversity of each destination, their love for each other deepening with every new experience.

In Paris, they strolled along the Seine River, hand in hand, taking in the romance of the city that had inspired countless love stories. Emi's eyes sparkled with creativity as she captured the essence of Parisian life in her sketches and paintings, while Akira found inspiration in the city's rich history and artistic heritage.

Their next stop was Venice, where they floated along the tranquil canals in a gondola, the city's unique charm casting a spell of enchantment over them. Emi's artistry flourished as she captured the city's beauty in watercolors, while Akira marveled at the intricate architecture and cultural richness that surrounded them.

In Florence, they wandered through museums and galleries, soaking in the masterpieces of Renaissance art and culture. Emi's passion for creativity was reignited, fueled by the timeless works of Michelangelo, Da Vinci, and Botticelli, while Akira found solace in the city's tranquil gardens and scenic vistas.

As they journeyed through Europe, Emi and Akira's love story unfolded against a backdrop of breathtaking landscapes, cultural discoveries, and shared moments of awe and wonder. They embraced each new experience with open hearts, knowing that every adventure deepened their bond and enriched their lives.

And so, as they bid farewell to Europe and boarded the plane back to Tokyo, Emi and Akira carried with them a treasure trove of memories—a testament to their love, their shared dreams, and the endless possibilities that awaited them on the journey of life together.

XXIV

Homecoming and Reflections

Returning to Tokyo after their European adventure filled Emi and Akira with a sense of nostalgia and reflection. The familiar streets welcomed them back with open arms, echoing the memories of their journey while reminding them of the beauty of home.

As they unpacked their suitcases and settled back into their routine, Emi and Akira found themselves immersed in a period of introspection. They looked through the sketches, paintings, and photographs they had brought back from their travels, each item a reminder of the moments they had shared and the lessons they had learned.

Emi's art had evolved during their time abroad, influenced by the sights, sounds, and emotions of their journey. She found inspiration in the fusion of cultures, incorporating new techniques and perspectives into her creations.

Akira, too, felt a shift in his mindset, his experiences in Europe sparking a renewed sense of creativity and exploration. He delved into new projects, blending elements of art, community, and innovation to bring his visions to life.

Their conversations became reflections on the transformative power of travel, the beauty of experiencing new cultures, and the importance of coming home to the people and places that shaped them.

As they sat on their balcony one evening, watching the city lights twinkle below, Emi spoke of her gratitude for the journey they had shared. She thanked Akira for being her constant companion and source of inspiration, for supporting her dreams and encouraging her growth.

Akira smiled, his eyes reflecting the love and admiration he felt for Emi. He expressed his own gratitude for the adventures they had embarked on together, for the memories they had created, and for the bond that had only grown stronger with each new experience.

And so, as they gazed out at the Tokyo skyline, Emi and Akira knew that their journey was far from over. It was a continuous cycle of exploration, growth, and love—a journey that would continue to unfold with each passing day, filled with the echoes of their adventures and the beauty of their shared life.

XXV

Seasons of Change

As Emi and Akira settled back into their routine in Tokyo, they found themselves embracing a new season of change—a time of growth, renewal, and exploration in both their personal and professional lives.

Emi's art studio flourished, attracting aspiring artists and enthusiasts alike. Her experiences in Europe had infused her work with a fresh perspective, drawing attention from galleries and collectors who were captivated by the unique blend of cultures and emotions in her creations.

Akira's community initiative expanded, bringing together a diverse group of individuals united by a common goal of making a positive impact in their neighborhoods. His vision of fostering creativity, collaboration, and social responsibility resonated with the community, inspiring meaningful projects and initiatives.

Their home became a hub of creativity and innovation, a space where ideas flourished and dreams took shape. Emi and Akira collaborated on projects that combined art, community engagement, and environmental sustainability, leaving a positive footprint on the world around them.

As the seasons changed once again, Emi and Akira reflected on the journey that had led them to this moment. They marveled at the beauty of growth, the resilience of their love, and the endless possibilities that lay ahead.

One evening, as they walked through a park ablaze with autumn colors, Emi turned to Akira with a smile. She spoke of their journey—the seasons of love, the dreams that bound them, and the legacy they were building together. She expressed her gratitude for his unwavering support and love, for being her partner in every adventure and every challenge.

Akira listened, his heart filled with love and admiration for Emi. He spoke of the joy she brought into his life, the way her passion and creativity inspired him, and the way their shared dreams had become a reality through their love and commitment to each other.

And so, as they embraced the changing seasons and the winds of change that whispered of new beginnings, Emi and Akira held hands, ready to embark on the next chapter of their journey together—a journey filled with love, laughter, growth, and the endless possibilities of a life lived with purpose and passion.

XXVI

Harmony of Hearts

Emi and Akira's journey continued to unfold, their lives intertwined in a harmony of hearts that echoed through every aspect of their existence. They found joy in the simplicity of everyday moments, in the shared laughter, and in the deep connection that bound them together.

As they explored new avenues of creativity and community engagement, Emi and Akira discovered a shared passion for music. They spent evenings listening to old records, dancing in their living room, and singing songs that spoke to their souls.

Music became a language of love for them—a way to express their emotions, dreams, and aspirations. Emi's voice blended harmoniously with Akira's guitar melodies, creating a symphony of sounds that resonated with the depth of their love.

Their love for music extended beyond their home, as they began performing at local events and collaborating with musicians who shared their vision of spreading joy and positivity through music.

One summer evening, as they performed under the starlit sky at a community concert, Emi looked at Akira with a twinkle in her eyes. She sang a song she had written, a tribute to their love story, capturing the journey they had shared and the dreams they had yet to fulfill.

Akira's guitar chords accompanied her words, weaving a melody of love, resilience, and hope. The audience was captivated by the emotion in their performance, feeling the warmth and sincerity of their connection.

After the concert, as they walked home hand in hand, Emi and Akira felt a sense of fulfillment and contentment. They knew that their love was not just a feeling but a melody that echoed through their hearts, creating a harmony that defined their relationship.

And so, as they sat on their balcony that night, listening to the gentle sounds of the city, Emi and Akira knew that their journey was far from over. It was a symphony of love, with each note representing a shared moment, a shared dream, and a shared lifetime of happiness and togetherness.

XXVII

Embracing Parenthood

Emi and Akira's love story took a new turn as they welcomed the arrival of their first child. The anticipation and excitement of becoming parents filled their hearts with a sense of wonder and joy, adding a new dimension to their already harmonious relationship.

As they prepared for the arrival of their baby, Emi and Akira embraced the journey of parenthood with open hearts and a shared sense of responsibility. They attended parenting classes together, read books on child development, and prepared their home to welcome their little one.

When the day finally arrived, and they held their baby in their arms for the first time, Emi and Akira's hearts swelled with love. They marveled at the miracle of life, the tiny fingers and toes, and the new bond that connected them as a family.

Parenthood brought new challenges and responsibilities, but Emi and Akira faced them together, supporting each other every step of the way. They took turns caring for their baby, sharing late-night feedings, and reveling in the joy of watching their child grow and thrive.

As they navigated the ups and downs of parenthood, Emi and Akira found that their love for each other deepened even further. They marveled at the strength and resilience of their relationship, knowing that their love was a solid foundation upon which they could build a happy and fulfilling family life.

Their home was filled with laughter, baby giggles, and the warmth of a love that had grown stronger with each passing day. Emi and Akira cherished every moment, knowing that they were creating cherished memories that would last a lifetime.

And so, as they sat in their living room one evening, watching their baby sleep peacefully, Emi and Akira felt a profound sense of gratitude and contentment. They knew that their journey of love had brought them to this beautiful moment of parenthood—a journey that they embraced with open hearts and a love that knew no bounds.

XXVIII
Navigating Challenges Together

As Emi and Akira settled into their roles as parents, they encountered challenges that tested their strength and resilience. Parenthood brought sleepless nights, moments of uncertainty, and new responsibilities that required patience and understanding.

One particularly challenging night, when their baby was teething and inconsolable, Emi and Akira found themselves exhausted and overwhelmed. But instead of letting the challenges divide them, they leaned on each other for support, offering words of encouragement and comfort.

They took turns soothing their baby, singing lullabies, and finding creative ways to ease the discomfort. Through their teamwork and unwavering love, they navigated the challenges together, strengthening their bond as a couple and as parents.

As their baby grew and reached new milestones, Emi and Akira faced new challenges with a sense of determination and unity. They celebrated the little victories, from first steps to first words, knowing that each moment was a testament to their love and dedication as parents.

Their journey was not without its ups and downs, but Emi and Akira faced each challenge with a sense of optimism and resilience. They learned to communicate openly, to seek support when needed, and to cherish the moments of joy and laughter that brightened their days.

Through it all, their love remained a constant—a source of strength and comfort that carried them through the highs and lows of parenthood. They knew that as long as they faced challenges together, with love and understanding, they could overcome anything life threw their way.

And so, as they watched their baby play happily in the living room one evening, Emi and Akira smiled at each other, their hearts filled with gratitude for the journey they had shared and the love that had carried them through every challenge. They knew that their love story was a testament to the power of love, resilience, and the beauty of navigating life's challenges together as a family.

XXIX

Rediscovering Romance

Amidst the whirlwind of parenthood and navigating life's challenges, Emi and Akira found moments to rediscover the romance that first brought them together. They recognized the importance of nurturing their relationship and making time for each other, even amidst the busyness of their lives.

One evening, they decided to have a special date night at home. They lit candles, prepared a delicious meal together, and set up a cozy spot in the living room where they could relax and reconnect.

As they enjoyed their meal and shared stories from their day, Emi and Akira felt a sense of closeness and intimacy that reminded them of the early days of their relationship. They laughed, reminisced about old memories, and expressed their love and appreciation for each other.

After dinner, they danced to their favorite songs, holding each other close and savoring the moments of togetherness. The music filled their home with warmth and romance, rekindling the passion and affection they had for each other.

Emi surprised Akira with a heartfelt letter expressing her love and gratitude for him as a partner and father. Akira, touched by her words, responded with his own heartfelt sentiments, reaffirming his love and commitment to their relationship.

Their date night was a reminder of the importance of keeping romance alive, even amidst the responsibilities of parenthood and daily life. Emi and Akira vowed to make more time for each other, to nurture their connection, and to continue creating moments of love and intimacy.

And so, as they curled up together on the couch, watching the stars twinkle through the window, Emi and Akira felt a renewed sense of love and closeness. They knew that their journey together was a beautiful tapestry woven with moments of love, laughter, challenges, and rediscovered romance—a journey that they cherished and celebrated with grateful hearts.

XXX

Celebrating Milestones

As Emi and Akira continued their journey of love, they found themselves celebrating milestones that marked their growth as individuals and as a couple. From personal achievements to shared experiences, each milestone was a testament to their love, resilience, and commitment to each other.

Emi's art career flourished, with her paintings gaining recognition in galleries and exhibitions. She received commissions for custom pieces and was invited to showcase her work in international art fairs, a testament to her talent and dedication to her craft.

Akira's community initiatives expanded, with new projects and collaborations that made a positive impact in their city. His vision of creating a better world through art, community engagement, and social responsibility gained traction, inspiring others to join in their efforts.

Together, they celebrated their wedding anniversary, reflecting on the years they had spent together and the love that had only grown stronger with time. They renewed their vows in a heartfelt ceremony surrounded by family and friends, reaffirming their commitment to each other and their shared dreams.

As their child grew and reached new milestones of their own, Emi and Akira found joy in witnessing their little one's journey of growth and discovery. They celebrated birthdays, holidays, and special moments as a family, cherishing the love and laughter that filled their home.

Their journey was not without challenges, but Emi and Akira faced them with resilience and determination, knowing that their love and support for each other would see them through any obstacle.

And so, as they gathered with loved ones to celebrate another milestone—a new art exhibition featuring Emi's latest works and Akira's community project reaching new heights—they felt a deep sense of gratitude and pride in how far they had come.

Their journey of love was a tapestry woven with threads of joy, resilience, passion, and shared dreams—a journey that they continued to embrace with open hearts and a love that knew no bounds.

XXXI

Finding Balance

Emi and Akira realized that amidst the celebrations and achievements, finding balance in their lives was crucial. They made a conscious effort to prioritize self-care, family time, and their relationship, recognizing that a harmonious balance was essential for their well-being and happiness.

They set aside dedicated moments for relaxation and rejuvenation, whether it was a quiet evening at home, a walk in nature, or a day of pampering at a spa. These moments of self-care allowed them to recharge and approach life's challenges with renewed energy and positivity.

Family time became a priority, with Emi and Akira creating traditions and routines that brought them closer together. From weekend outings to family movie nights, they cherished the moments spent bonding and creating memories with their child.

Their relationship also flourished as they made time for date nights, heartfelt conversations, and shared activities that reignited the spark of romance and connection. They communicated openly, expressing their needs and desires, and deepened their understanding and appreciation for each other.

As they navigated the demands of work, family, and personal growth, Emi and Akira found that finding balance was an ongoing journey—one that required mindfulness, communication, and a willingness to prioritize what truly mattered.

They celebrated not only the big moments but also the small victories, acknowledging each step forward in their quest for balance and harmony. Whether it was a successful art exhibition, a meaningful community project, or simply a peaceful evening at home, they found joy in the journey itself.

And so, as they looked ahead to the future with optimism and gratitude, Emi and Akira knew that their journey of love was not just about achieving goals but also about finding balance, nurturing relationships, and savoring the beauty of each moment, one step at a time.

XXXII
Embracing Change I

Emi and Akira's journey took an unexpected turn when they faced a significant change in their lives. Akira received an opportunity to work on a global project that required them to relocate temporarily to a different country.

At first, the idea of uprooting their lives and moving to a new place seemed daunting. Emi and Akira discussed the potential challenges and uncertainties, but they also saw it as an opportunity for growth, adventure, and new experiences.

They embraced the change with open hearts, viewing it as a chance to expand their horizons, meet new people, and immerse themselves in a different culture. They packed their belongings, said goodbye to their home in Tokyo, and embarked on a new chapter together.

The transition to a new country brought its share of challenges, from adjusting to a different language and lifestyle to navigating unfamiliar surroundings. But Emi and Akira faced these challenges as a team, supporting each other and finding strength in their bond.

As they settled into their new home, Emi's art continued to flourish, inspired by the sights, sounds, and colors of their new environment. Akira's global project provided opportunities for collaboration and innovation, allowing him to expand his network and contribute to meaningful initiatives on a larger scale.

Their child adapted to the changes with resilience, making new friends, learning a new language, and embracing the adventure of living in a new country.

Through it all, Emi and Akira found that change brought growth, resilience, and a deeper appreciation for the journey they were on together. They embraced the unknown with curiosity and courage, knowing that every experience, whether challenging or rewarding, was a stepping stone in their journey of love and discovery.

And so, as they navigated the changes and uncertainties of their new chapter, Emi and Akira faced each day with optimism, gratitude, and a sense of adventure, knowing that their love was a constant anchor that guided them through life's ever-changing landscapes.

XXXIII

Embracing Diversity

Emi and Akira's relocation to a new country opened their eyes to the beauty of diversity and the richness of different cultures. They embraced the opportunity to learn and immerse themselves in the traditions, customs, and perspectives of their new community.

They attended cultural festivals, tried new cuisines, and made friends from various backgrounds, deepening their understanding of the world and broadening their horizons.

Emi's art took on new dimensions as she drew inspiration from the diverse landscapes, people, and stories around her. Her paintings reflected the vibrant colors, textures, and emotions of their new environment, capturing the essence of cultural diversity in her art.

Akira's work on the global project allowed him to collaborate with individuals from different countries, bridging cultural gaps and fostering a spirit of collaboration and unity. His experiences taught him the value of diversity and the power of inclusivity in creating positive change.

Their child thrived in this multicultural environment, embracing diversity with open arms, learning from different perspectives, and growing into a global citizen with a deep appreciation for the beauty of cultural differences.

As they navigated the complexities and joys of living in a diverse community, Emi and Akira found that their love for each other and their shared values of acceptance, respect, and empathy were the pillars that strengthened their connection amidst the tapestry of diversity.

They celebrated holidays from different cultures, shared stories and traditions with their new friends, and embraced the beauty of a world where differences were celebrated and cherished.

And so, as they looked around at the diverse tapestry of their lives, Emi and Akira felt grateful for the opportunity to embrace diversity, to learn from each other, and to contribute to a world where love, acceptance, and understanding bridged cultural divides. Their journey continued to be a celebration of unity in diversity, a testament to the beauty of a life enriched by the mosaic of cultures and perspectives that surrounded them.

XXXIV

A Tapestry of Resilience

Amidst the beauty of diversity and the challenges of adapting to a new country, Emi and Akira faced a test of resilience that strengthened their bond and deepened their connection. They encountered unexpected hurdles, from language barriers to cultural differences, but they faced each challenge with determination and a spirit of unity.

Emi's art became a reflection of their journey of resilience, capturing the emotions, struggles, and triumphs of overcoming obstacles and embracing change. Her paintings told stories of resilience, hope, and the beauty of resilience in the face of adversity.

Akira's work on the global project also required resilience, as he navigated complex negotiations, cultural nuances, and unexpected setbacks. His ability to adapt, collaborate, and lead with empathy became a source of inspiration for his team and the community they served.

Their child witnessed their resilience firsthand, learning valuable lessons about perseverance, adaptability, and the strength that comes from facing challenges with courage and determination.

As they reflected on their journey of resilience, Emi and Akira realized that their love and partnership were the foundation that allowed them to weather storms and emerge stronger together. They found strength in each other's support, encouragement, and unwavering belief in their ability to overcome any obstacle.

Their journey was a tapestry woven with threads of resilience, love, and determination—a testament to the power of unity in the face of adversity. They celebrated their triumphs, learned from their challenges, and continued to grow individually and as a couple through every experience.

And so, as they looked back at the hurdles they had overcome and the lessons they had learned, Emi and Akira knew that their journey of resilience was a testament to the depth of their love, the strength of their partnership, and the beauty of a life lived with courage, resilience, and unwavering faith in each other.

XXXV

The Power of Gratitude

Emi and Akira's journey of resilience led them to a profound realization—the power of gratitude in transforming challenges into opportunities and setbacks into stepping stones. They began to cultivate a daily practice of gratitude, acknowledging and appreciating the blessings, lessons, and moments of joy in their lives.

Emi expressed gratitude for the beauty she found in everyday moments—the warmth of a sunrise, the laughter of their child, the comfort of a shared meal. She channeled this gratitude into her art, infusing her paintings with a sense of appreciation for life's simple pleasures.

Akira embraced gratitude for the strength and resilience they had shown as a couple and as a family. He expressed gratitude for the love and support they received from their community, for the opportunities to make a positive impact, and for the journey that had brought them to where they were.

Their child learned the power of gratitude through their example, expressing thanks for the small kindnesses, the moments of learning, and the love that surrounded them each day.

As they embraced gratitude, Emi and Akira noticed a shift in their perspective—they saw challenges as opportunities for growth, setbacks as lessons in resilience, and moments of joy as gifts to be cherished.

Their journey became a celebration of gratitude, a recognition of the abundance that filled their lives, and a reminder of the importance of counting blessings amidst life's ups and downs.

And so, as they sat together one evening, watching the sunset paint the sky in hues of gold and pink, Emi and Akira felt a deep sense of gratitude for the journey they had shared—the challenges, the triumphs, and the moments of love and connection that had shaped their lives. They knew that gratitude was not just a feeling but a way of life—a practice that enriched their journey, deepened their bond, and filled their hearts with joy and contentment.

XXXVI

Embracing New Beginnings

As Emi and Akira continued their journey filled with resilience and gratitude, they found themselves at a crossroads—a moment of new beginnings and fresh opportunities. They reflected on the lessons they had learned, the growth they had experienced, and the love that had carried them through every challenge.

With a sense of anticipation and excitement, they embarked on new adventures and pursued new passions. Emi explored new artistic styles, pushing the boundaries of her creativity and expressing her evolving perspectives through her art.

Akira delved into new projects that aligned with his values and aspirations, leveraging his skills and experience to make a positive impact in areas that mattered most to him. He embraced innovation, collaboration, and continuous learning as he navigated new opportunities.

Their child, now a curious and adventurous soul, embraced new experiences with enthusiasm and a sense of wonder. They discovered new hobbies, made new friends, and embraced the joys of learning and discovery.

As they embraced new beginnings, Emi and Akira carried with them the lessons of resilience, gratitude, and love that had guided them through their journey. They approached each new chapter with open hearts, a spirit of curiosity, and a belief in the endless possibilities that lay ahead.

Their journey of love continued to unfold, weaving together moments of joy, growth, and connection. They celebrated milestones, embraced challenges, and embraced the beauty of living fully in each moment.

And so, as they looked towards the horizon of new beginnings, Emi and Akira felt a sense of excitement and anticipation for the adventures that awaited them. They knew that their journey was a tapestry woven with threads of resilience, gratitude, and love—a journey that would continue to inspire, uplift, and fill their lives with meaning and purpose.

XXXVII

Nurturing Connections

Emi and Akira's journey of new beginnings led them to a deeper appreciation for the importance of nurturing connections—with each other, their family, friends, and the world around them. They realized that meaningful connections were the fabric that wove their lives together, enriching their experiences and shaping their journey.

They prioritized quality time with loved ones, organizing gatherings, and moments of togetherness that strengthened their bonds. Whether it was a cozy dinner with family, a fun outing with friends, or a heartfelt conversation with a loved one, they cherished the connections that added warmth and depth to their lives.

Emi's art became a medium for fostering connections, as she collaborated with fellow artists, shared her work with the community, and used her talent to spread messages of unity, compassion, and understanding.

Akira continued his work in community engagement, creating spaces for meaningful conversations, collaborations, and initiatives that brought people together and fostered a sense of belonging and connection.

Their child learned the value of connections through their experiences, forming friendships, developing empathy, and appreciating the beauty of human connection in all its forms.

As they nurtured connections in their lives, Emi and Akira found that their journey was enriched by the love, support, and shared experiences they had with others. They realized that connections were not just about being together physically but also about being present, listening, and sharing moments of joy, laughter, and vulnerability.

And so, as they sat around a table filled with laughter and shared stories, Emi and Akira felt a deep sense of gratitude for the connections that had shaped their journey. They knew that their lives were enriched by the love, laughter, and connections they had nurtured along the way—a tapestry of connections that made their journey of love and discovery truly meaningful and fulfilling.

XXXVIII

Cultivating Compassion

Emi and Akira's journey of nurturing connections led them to a profound understanding of the importance of compassion—in their relationships, in their interactions with others, and in their approach to life's challenges. They realized that compassion was the key to deepening their connections, fostering empathy, and creating a more compassionate world.

They practiced compassion in their daily lives, offering kindness, understanding, and support to those around them. Whether it was lending a listening ear to a friend in need, extending a helping hand to a stranger, or showing patience and empathy in moments of conflict, they embodied the spirit of compassion in their actions.

Emi's art became a medium for spreading compassion, as she created pieces that evoked emotions, sparked conversations, and inspired reflection on the beauty of empathy, kindness, and understanding.

Akira's work in community engagement took on a new dimension as he advocated for compassion-driven initiatives, promoted dialogue and understanding among diverse groups, and championed causes that supported the most vulnerable members of society.

Their child learned the value of compassion through their parents' example, growing into a compassionate and empathetic individual who sought to make a positive difference in the world.

As they cultivated compassion in their lives, Emi and Akira found that their connections deepened, their relationships strengthened, and their sense of fulfillment grew. They realized that compassion was not just a virtue but a way of life—a way of seeing the world with empathy, kindness, and a willingness to make a difference.

And so, as they reflected on their journey of nurturing connections and cultivating compassion, Emi and Akira felt a sense of purpose and joy. They knew that their journey was not just about their own growth and happiness but also about spreading compassion, making a positive impact, and leaving a legacy of love and kindness for future generations—a legacy that would continue to inspire, uplift, and transform lives for years to come.

XXXIX

Embracing Imperfection

Emi and Akira's journey of cultivating compassion led them to a deeper understanding of the beauty of imperfection—in themselves, in their relationships, and in the world around them. They realized that imperfections were not flaws but unique aspects that added depth, character, and authenticity to their lives.

They embraced their own imperfections with self-compassion, learning to be kinder to themselves, to embrace their vulnerabilities, and to celebrate their strengths and quirks. Through this acceptance, they found inner peace, confidence, and a greater sense of self-love.

In their relationships, Emi and Akira embraced imperfections as opportunities for growth, learning, and deeper connection. They communicated openly, addressed conflicts with empathy and understanding, and celebrated the beauty of unconditional love that accepted each other's imperfections wholeheartedly.

Emi's art reflected this embrace of imperfection, as she explored themes of vulnerability, resilience, and self-acceptance in her paintings. Her work resonated with others who found solace, inspiration, and a sense of belonging in the beauty of imperfection.

Akira's work in community engagement took on a new dimension as he advocated for inclusivity, diversity, and acceptance of differences. He promoted dialogue, understanding, and empathy, creating spaces where imperfections were embraced as opportunities for connection and growth.

Their child learned the importance of embracing imperfections as part of the human experience, growing into a confident, compassionate individual who celebrated their uniqueness and valued authenticity in themselves and others.

As they embraced imperfection in their lives, Emi and Akira found that their relationships deepened, their creativity flourished, and their sense of fulfillment grew. They realized that imperfection was not a sign of weakness but a testament to the beauty of being human—flawed, vulnerable, and beautifully imperfect.

And so, as they looked at their journey of embracing imperfection with gratitude and acceptance, Emi and Akira felt a profound sense of wholeness and authenticity. They knew that their journey was a celebration of imperfection—a journey that honored the beauty of being true to oneself, embracing vulnerabilities, and finding strength and beauty in the imperfect moments of life.

XL

Embracing Change II

Emi and Akira's journey of embracing imperfection led them to a deeper understanding of the inevitability of change—in themselves, in their relationships, and in the world around them. They realized that change was a constant in life, and embracing it with openness, adaptability, and resilience was key to navigating life's ever-evolving landscapes.

They embraced change as an opportunity for growth, learning, and transformation. Instead of resisting or fearing change, they approached it with curiosity, courage, and a willingness to embrace new possibilities.

In their relationships, Emi and Akira navigated changes with grace and understanding. They communicated openly, supported each other through transitions, and embraced the evolution of their connection as they grew individually and as a couple.

Emi's art reflected this embrace of change, as she explored themes of transformation, renewal, and the beauty of letting go in her paintings. Her work resonated with others who found inspiration and solace in the fluidity of life's journey.

Akira's work in community engagement also evolved as he adapted to changing dynamics, emerging needs, and new opportunities. He remained agile, innovative, and proactive in his approach, seeking creative solutions and fostering collaboration in the face of change.

Their child learned the value of adaptability and resilience as they navigated transitions, embraced new experiences, and learned from the ebb and flow of life's changes.

As they embraced change in their lives, Emi and Akira found that their capacity for growth, creativity, and joy expanded. They realized that change was not something to be feared but a natural part of the journey—a catalyst for new beginnings, discoveries, and possibilities.

And so, as they reflected on their journey of embracing change with courage and openness, Emi and Akira felt a deep sense of gratitude for the richness of experiences, lessons learned, and the beauty of a life lived fully in the embrace of change. They knew that their journey was a testament to the resilience of the human spirit, the beauty of transformation, and the infinite potential that comes with embracing the ever-changing tapestry of life.

XLI

Finding Balance

Emi and Akira's journey of embracing change led them to a newfound appreciation for the importance of balance—in their lives, in their relationships, and in their pursuit of passion and purpose. They realized that finding equilibrium was key to navigating the complexities of life with harmony, clarity, and inner peace.

They prioritized self-care and well-being, carving out time for rest, relaxation, and activities that nourished their minds, bodies, and souls. Whether it was practicing mindfulness, engaging in physical exercise, or pursuing hobbies that brought them joy, they embraced the importance of balance in maintaining their overall well-being.

In their relationships, Emi and Akira cultivated balance by honoring each other's needs, boundaries, and aspirations. They communicated openly, listened with empathy, and made decisions together that supported their mutual growth and happiness.

Emi's art reflected this pursuit of balance, as she explored themes of harmony, serenity, and the beauty of finding equilibrium amidst life's ups and downs. Her paintings resonated with others who sought a sense of balance and tranquility in a busy world.

Akira's work in community engagement also reflected a balanced approach, as he sought to create inclusive spaces, foster collaboration, and prioritize the well-being of those he served.

Their child learned the value of balance as they observed their parents' commitment to self-care, healthy boundaries, and a balanced lifestyle. They embraced a sense of equilibrium in their own activities, relationships, and pursuits.

As they found balance in their lives, Emi and Akira felt a sense of harmony, clarity, and fulfillment. They realized that balance was not about perfection but about navigating life's challenges with resilience, adaptability, and a grounded sense of self.

And so, as they reflected on their journey of finding balance, Emi and Akira felt grateful for the peace and wholeness that came with honoring the interconnected aspects of their lives. They knew that their journey was a continual exploration of equilibrium—a dance between responsibilities and passions, challenges and joys, growth and serenity—a journey that they embraced with gratitude, wisdom, and a deep appreciation for the beauty of balance.

XLII
Embracing Self-Discovery

Emi and Akira's journey of finding balance led them on a path of self-discovery—a journey of exploring their passions, values, and deepest desires. They realized that self-discovery was an ongoing process of introspection, growth, and aligning their lives with their authentic selves.

They dedicated time to self-reflection, journaling, and mindfulness practices that allowed them to connect with their inner wisdom, aspirations, and dreams. Through this process, they gained clarity on what mattered most to them and took steps to align their actions with their values and goals.

In their relationships, Emi and Akira embraced self-discovery as a shared journey, supporting each other's personal growth, aspirations, and exploration of new interests. They celebrated each other's strengths, encouraged creative expression, and fostered an environment of acceptance and growth.

Emi's art became a reflection of her self-discovery journey, as she expressed her innermost thoughts, emotions, and revelations through her paintings. Her work evolved as she delved deeper into her artistic voice and explored new avenues of creativity.

Akira's work in community engagement also reflected his journey of self-discovery, as he aligned his efforts with causes that resonated with his values and passion for creating positive change. He leveraged his strengths, skills, and insights to make a meaningful impact in areas that aligned with his authentic self.

Their child embraced self-discovery through exploration, curiosity, and a sense of wonder about the world and their own potential. They learned to trust their instincts, embrace their uniqueness, and pursue their interests with passion and confidence.

As they embraced self-discovery in their lives, Emi and Akira felt a deep sense of fulfillment, purpose, and authenticity. They realized that self-discovery was not a destination but a continual journey of growth, learning, and becoming more fully themselves.

And so, as they looked ahead to the future with excitement and curiosity, Emi and Akira knew that their journey of self-discovery was a testament to the beauty of embracing who they were, honoring their truths, and living authentically in alignment with their values and passions.

XLIII

Embracing Gratitude

Emi and Akira's journey of self-discovery led them to a profound appreciation for the power of gratitude—in their lives, relationships, and the world around them. They realized that gratitude was a transformative force that enriched every aspect of their journey, fostering joy, resilience, and a deep sense of connection.

They cultivated a daily practice of gratitude, taking time each day to reflect on the blessings, lessons, and moments of beauty that filled their lives. They expressed gratitude for the love they shared, the challenges that helped them grow, and the simple pleasures that brought them happiness.

In their relationships, Emi and Akira expressed gratitude openly, acknowledging the support, kindness, and love they received from each other and their loved ones. They communicated their appreciation regularly, strengthening their bonds and deepening their connection.

Emi's art reflected this embrace of gratitude, as she infused her paintings with themes of appreciation, abundance, and the beauty of gratitude in everyday moments. Her work resonated with others who found inspiration and joy in the practice of gratitude.

Akira's work in community engagement also emphasized gratitude, as he encouraged a culture of appreciation, recognition, and celebration of achievements and contributions within the community.

Their child learned the value of gratitude through their parents' example, expressing thanks for the people, experiences, and opportunities that enriched their lives.

As they embraced gratitude in their lives, Emi and Akira felt a profound sense of joy, fulfillment, and contentment. They realized that gratitude was not just a feeling but a way of living—a practice that transformed challenges into opportunities, setbacks into lessons, and moments of joy into cherished memories.

And so, as they looked around at the abundance of blessings in their lives, Emi and Akira felt a deep sense of gratitude for the journey they had shared—the ups and downs, the growth and learning, and the love that had sustained them through it all. They knew that their journey of gratitude was a celebration of life's richness, a testament to the beauty of being present, and a reminder of the power of gratitude to transform lives and hearts.

XLIV

Embracing Resilience

Emi and Akira's journey of embracing gratitude continued to evolve as they encountered new challenges and opportunities for growth. They realized that resilience was an essential companion on their journey—a quality that allowed them to navigate obstacles, bounce back from setbacks, and emerge stronger and wiser.

They embraced resilience by cultivating a mindset of optimism, adaptability, and perseverance. They faced challenges with courage, viewed failures as stepping stones to success, and learned valuable lessons from every experience.

In their relationships, Emi and Akira demonstrated resilience by supporting each other through tough times, offering encouragement, and finding strength in their shared love and commitment. They communicated openly, worked through challenges together, and celebrated their ability to overcome obstacles as a team.

Emi's art reflected this embrace of resilience, as she explored themes of resilience, inner strength, and the beauty of rising above adversity in her paintings. Her work resonated with others who found inspiration and hope in the message of resilience.

Akira's work in community engagement also emphasized resilience, as he advocated for resources, support, and initiatives that empowered individuals and communities to bounce back from adversity and thrive.

Their child learned the value of resilience through their parents' example, facing challenges with courage, learning from setbacks, and developing a resilient mindset that served them well in life.

As they embraced resilience in their lives, Emi and Akira felt a deep sense of empowerment, confidence, and determination. They realized that resilience was not just about bouncing back but about growing stronger, gaining wisdom, and embracing the journey with courage and resilience.

And so, as they looked ahead to the future with optimism and resilience, Emi and Akira knew that their journey of embracing resilience was a testament to their inner strength, their unwavering belief in themselves and each other, and their ability to thrive in the face of challenges. They knew that with resilience as their companion, they could continue to navigate life's ups and downs with grace, courage, and a spirit of resilience.

XLV

Embracing Change III

Emi and Akira's journey of resilience and gratitude led them to a profound understanding of the inevitability of change. They realized that change was not something to be feared but embraced—a catalyst for growth, transformation, and new beginnings.

They embraced change by adopting a mindset of flexibility, adaptability, and curiosity. Instead of resisting change, they approached it with open hearts and minds, welcoming the opportunities it brought for learning, exploration, and personal evolution.

In their relationships, Emi and Akira navigated change with grace and understanding, supporting each other through transitions, and embracing the opportunities for growth and deeper connection that change brought.

Emi's art reflected this embrace of change, as she explored themes of transformation, renewal, and the beauty of letting go in her paintings. Her work resonated with others who found inspiration and solace in the fluidity of life's journey.

Akira's work in community engagement also evolved as he adapted to changing dynamics, emerging needs, and new opportunities. He remained agile, innovative, and proactive in his approach, seeking creative solutions and fostering collaboration in the face of change.

Their child learned the value of adaptability and resilience as they navigated transitions, embraced new experiences, and learned from the ebb and flow of life's changes.

As they embraced change in their lives, Emi and Akira felt a sense of liberation, growth, and renewal. They realized that change was not a disruption but a natural part of the journey—a doorway to new experiences, discoveries, and possibilities.

And so, as they looked ahead to the horizon of new beginnings with excitement and anticipation, Emi and Akira knew that their journey of embracing change was a testament to their courage, resilience, and willingness to embrace the ever-changing tapestry of life. They knew that with each change, they grew stronger, wiser, and more deeply connected to the beauty and possibilities that lay ahead.

XLVI

Embracing Transformation

Emi and Akira's journey of embracing change continued to unfold as they delved deeper into the transformative power of their experiences. They realized that change was not just about external shifts but also about internal transformations—a journey of growth, self-discovery, and evolving into their best selves.

They embraced transformation by cultivating a mindset of curiosity, self-reflection, and a willingness to let go of old patterns that no longer served them. They embraced the process of change as an opportunity to evolve, learn, and become more aligned with their authentic selves.

In their relationships, Emi and Akira explored transformation together, supporting each other's personal growth, aspirations, and exploration of new paths. They celebrated each other's progress, encouraged self-expression, and nurtured a space where transformation was welcomed and embraced.

Emi's art reflected this journey of transformation, as she delved into new styles, themes, and mediums that allowed her creativity to flourish and evolve. Her work resonated with others who found inspiration and empowerment in the message of transformation and growth.

Akira's work in community engagement also reflected this spirit of transformation, as he sought to create spaces and initiatives that empowered individuals and communities to embrace change, learn from it, and grow stronger together.

Their child learned the value of transformation through their parents' example, witnessing the beauty and possibilities that came with embracing change, learning from experiences, and evolving into the person they were meant to be.

As they embraced transformation in their lives, Emi and Akira felt a sense of liberation, empowerment, and renewal. They realized that transformation was a continual journey—a process of shedding old layers, embracing new insights, and stepping into the fullness of their potential.

And so, as they looked ahead with excitement and curiosity, Emi and Akira knew that their journey of embracing transformation was a testament to their resilience, courage, and commitment to growth. They knew that with each transformation, they became more aligned with their true selves and the possibilities that awaited them on their journey.

XLVII

Embracing Connection

Emi and Akira's journey of transformation led them to a deeper appreciation for the power of connection—in their relationships, in their work, and in their connection to the world around them. They realized that meaningful connections were the foundation of a fulfilling life, enriching their experiences and bringing a sense of purpose and belonging.

They embraced connection by fostering authentic relationships, cultivating empathy, and actively seeking opportunities to connect with others on a deeper level. They prioritized quality time with loved ones, engaged in meaningful conversations, and supported each other through life's ups and downs.

In their work, Emi and Akira emphasized the importance of connection, creating spaces and initiatives that fostered collaboration, understanding, and a sense of community. They recognized the power of connection in creating positive change, fostering creativity, and inspiring growth.

Emi's art reflected this embrace of connection, as she explored themes of unity, empathy, and the beauty of human connection in her paintings. Her work resonated with others who found solace, inspiration, and a sense of belonging in the message of connection.

Akira's work in community engagement also centered around connection, as he facilitated dialogue, promoted inclusivity, and created opportunities for people to come together, share their stories, and forge meaningful connections.

Their child learned the value of connection through their parents' example, developing strong bonds with family and friends, and embracing the beauty of connection in all its forms.

As they embraced connection in their lives, Emi and Akira felt a deep sense of fulfillment, joy, and purpose. They realized that connection was not just about being together but about truly seeing, understanding, and supporting each other on their journey.

And so, as they looked around at the web of connections that enriched their lives, Emi and Akira felt grateful for the depth of relationships, the moments of shared laughter and tears, and the sense of belonging that came with embracing connection. They knew that their journey of connection was a celebration of the human experience—a journey of love, growth, and the beauty of being deeply connected to oneself and others.

XLVIII
Embracing Joy

Emi and Akira's journey of connection continued to evolve as they embraced the essence of joy—finding delight in the simple moments, cultivating gratitude for life's blessings, and infusing their days with laughter and lightness. They realized that joy was not just an emotion but a way of being—a state of mind that radiated positivity, resilience, and a deep appreciation for life.

They embraced joy by savoring the present moment, practicing mindfulness, and choosing to focus on the beauty and goodness that surrounded them. They found joy in the little things—a shared smile, a heartfelt conversation, a moment of quiet reflection—and allowed these moments to fill their hearts with happiness.

In their relationships, Emi and Akira shared joy with loved ones, creating memories filled with laughter, love, and warmth. They celebrated milestones, cherished traditions, and embraced spontaneity, finding joy in the connections they nurtured and the experiences they shared.

Emi's art reflected this embrace of joy, as she captured moments of beauty, happiness, and whimsy in her paintings. Her work resonated with others who found joy and inspiration in the vibrant colors, playful themes, and uplifting messages conveyed through her art.

Akira's work in community engagement also centered around joy, as he organized events, initiatives, and programs that brought people together in celebration, fostering a sense of unity, connection, and shared joy within the community.

Their child learned the value of joy through their parents' example, experiencing the wonder and magic of life's simple pleasures, and embracing a mindset of positivity and gratitude.

As they embraced joy in their lives, Emi and Akira felt a deep sense of contentment, fulfillment, and inner peace. They realized that joy was not dependent on external circumstances but a choice they made each day—to find beauty in the ordinary, to spread kindness and laughter, and to embrace life with an open heart and a joyful spirit.

And so, as they looked ahead with anticipation and gratitude, Emi and Akira knew that their journey of embracing joy was a testament to their resilience, their capacity for love, and their deep appreciation for the richness of life's experiences. They knew that with joy as their guiding light, they could navigate life's ups and downs with grace, laughter, and a heart full of joy.

XLIX
Embracing Fulfillment

Emi and Akira's journey of embracing joy continued to unfold as they delved deeper into the essence of fulfillment—finding meaning, purpose, and a sense of completeness in their lives. They realized that true fulfillment came from aligning their actions with their values, pursuing their passions, and contributing positively to the world around them.

They embraced fulfillment by living with intention, clarity, and a deep sense of purpose. They identified what mattered most to them, set meaningful goals, and took inspired action to bring their visions to life.

In their relationships, Emi and Akira nurtured fulfillment by cultivating deep connections, mutual support, and shared experiences that enriched their lives and the lives of those around them. They celebrated achievements, supported each other's dreams, and found fulfillment in the love and connection they shared.

Emi's art reflected this embrace of fulfillment, as she expressed her innermost dreams, aspirations, and values through her paintings. Her work inspired others to pursue their passions, follow their hearts, and find fulfillment in expressing their unique gifts and perspectives.

Akira's work in community engagement also centered around fulfillment, as he collaborated with others to create initiatives, programs, and projects that made a positive impact, fostered a sense of belonging, and contributed to the well-being of the community.

Their child learned the value of fulfillment through their parents' example, witnessing the joy and satisfaction that came from living authentically, pursuing passions, and making a difference in the lives of others.

As they embraced fulfillment in their lives, Emi and Akira felt a deep sense of satisfaction, purpose, and inner peace. They realized that fulfillment was not about external validation or achievements but about living in alignment with their true selves, making meaningful contributions, and nurturing loving connections.

And so, as they looked back on their journey with gratitude and pride, Emi and Akira knew that their journey of embracing fulfillment was a testament to their courage, resilience, and unwavering commitment to living a life of purpose and passion. They knew that with fulfillment as their compass, they could continue to inspire, uplift, and make a positive impact in the world around them, leaving a legacy of love, joy, and fulfillment for generations to come.

L

Embracing Love

Emi and Akira's journey of fulfillment culminated in a profound realization—the ultimate essence of life was love. They understood that love was the thread that connected their entire journey, weaving through every experience, every emotion, and every connection they had encountered.

They embraced love as the foundation of their lives, nurturing it in their relationships, their work, and their interactions with the world. They realized that love was not just a feeling but a way of being—a choice they made each day to show kindness, compassion, and understanding.

In their relationships, Emi and Akira cultivated love by prioritizing empathy, communication, and mutual respect. They celebrated each other's uniqueness, supported each other's growth, and found joy in the deep connection and love they shared.

Emi's art became a manifestation of love, as she expressed the beauty, depth, and complexity of human emotions through her paintings. Her work touched hearts, evoking feelings of love, joy, and connection in those who experienced it.

Akira's work in community engagement also reflected the power of love, as he worked tirelessly to create a world where everyone felt valued, accepted, and loved for who they were.

Their child learned the value of love through their parents' example, experiencing firsthand the warmth, acceptance, and security that love brought into their lives.

As they embraced love in its fullest expression, Emi and Akira felt a deep sense of gratitude, fulfillment, and peace. They realized that love was the essence of their journey—a journey of growth, resilience, joy, and ultimately, love.

And so, as they looked back on their 50-book journey titled "Love Stories Around the World," Emi and Akira knew that their own love story—the story of Sophie and Alex in "First Love in Paris" and their journey through ups and downs, challenges and triumphs, growth and fulfillment—was a reflection of the universal truth that love conquers all, binds us together, and transforms lives in ways we can never imagine.

Their journey was a celebration of love in all its forms—a testament to the beauty, power, and enduring nature of love that transcends boundaries, cultures, and time itself. And as they looked ahead to the future with hearts full of love, Emi and Akira knew that their journey was just the beginning of a lifetime of love, growth, and endless possibilities.

LI

Embracing Endings and Beginnings

As Emi and Akira reflected on their 50-book journey of love, they realized that every story had an ending, but it also marked the beginning of something new. They embraced the bittersweet beauty of endings and the excitement of new beginnings, understanding that life was a continuous cycle of endings leading to fresh starts.

In their own lives, Emi and Akira embraced endings with gratitude and reflection, honoring the lessons, memories, and growth that each chapter had brought. They acknowledged the beauty of closure, letting go of what no longer served them, and making space for new experiences and possibilities.

In their relationships, Emi and Akira navigated endings with compassion and understanding, recognizing that sometimes letting go was an act of love and growth. They cherished the memories, celebrated the journey, and embraced the transitions that came with endings, knowing that new beginnings awaited.

Emi's art reflected this embrace of endings and beginnings, as she captured the beauty of transitions, cycles, and the natural ebb and flow of life in her paintings. Her work resonated with others who found solace, inspiration, and hope in the cycles of life.

Akira's work in community engagement also centered around endings and beginnings, as he facilitated processes, programs, and initiatives that supported individuals and communities through transitions, changes, and new chapters.

Their child learned the value of endings and beginnings through their parents' example, navigating transitions with resilience, grace, and an open heart.

As Emi and Akira embraced the ending of their 50-book journey, they felt a mix of emotions—gratitude for the experiences, pride in their growth, and excitement for what lay ahead. They knew that every ending marked a new beginning—a fresh canvas to paint new stories, explore new adventures, and continue their journey of love, growth, and fulfillment.

And so, as they looked ahead to the next chapter of their lives, Emi and Akira embraced endings and beginnings with open arms, knowing that the journey of love was infinite, ever-evolving, and filled with endless possibilities waiting to be discovered.

LII

Embracing Legacy

As Emi and Akira embarked on the next chapter of their lives, they reflected on the legacy they wanted to leave behind—a legacy of love, compassion, and positive impact on the world. They understood that legacy was not just about what they achieved but about the lives they touched, the hearts they inspired, and the values they embodied.

They embraced the concept of legacy by living with integrity, authenticity, and a commitment to making a difference in the lives of others. They sought to leave behind a world that was more compassionate, inclusive, and filled with love.

In their relationships, Emi and Akira focused on nurturing meaningful connections, leaving behind a legacy of love, support, and understanding. They shared their wisdom, experiences, and values with the next generation, ensuring that their legacy of love continued to flourish.

Emi's art became a part of their legacy, as her paintings inspired others to embrace beauty, creativity, and the power of expression. Her work left a lasting impact, touching hearts and souls long after she was gone.

Akira's work in community engagement also contributed to their legacy, as he created initiatives, programs, and movements that created positive change, empowered individuals, and built a legacy of unity and connection within communities.

Their child inherited their legacy, carrying forward the values of love, compassion, and making a difference in the world. They became stewards of the legacy, continuing the journey of love and impact that Emi and Akira had started.

As Emi and Akira looked back on their journey, they felt a deep sense of fulfillment knowing that their legacy of love would continue to inspire, uplift, and bring positive change to the world. They understood that legacy was not about the past but about the future—a future they had helped shape through their love, passion, and commitment to leaving the world a better place than they found it.

And so, as they embraced their legacy with open hearts and gratitude, Emi and Akira knew that their journey of love was timeless, eternal, and a testament to the enduring power of love to transform lives and leave a legacy that would be remembered for generations to come.

LIII

Embracing Reflection

As Emi and Akira approached the culmination of their journey, they took time for deep reflection. They looked back on the experiences, lessons, and moments that had shaped their lives, recognizing the growth, challenges, and joys that had woven their story together.

In their reflection, Emi and Akira found gratitude for the journey they had traveled—the highs and lows, the laughter and tears, and the love that had sustained them through it all. They acknowledged the impact of their choices, the power of their relationships, and the resilience that had carried them forward.

Reflecting on their legacy, Emi and Akira felt a sense of pride in the love they had cultivated, the connections they had nurtured, and the positive impact they had made on the world. They understood that their journey was not just their own but a tapestry woven with the threads of love, compassion, and the shared human experience.

Their reflection deepened their appreciation for each other, for their family, and for the community that had supported them along the way. They realized that every moment, every choice, and every connection had contributed to the richness and depth of their journey.

And so, as they embraced reflection, Emi and Akira felt a sense of completion—a readiness to honor the past, cherish the present, and step into the future with gratitude and a heart full of love.

LIV
Embracing Gratitude

In the final stretch of their journey, Emi and Akira found themselves overwhelmed with gratitude. They reflected on the countless blessings, the moments of joy, the challenges that had shaped them, and the love that had sustained them throughout their adventure.

They expressed gratitude for each other—for the unwavering support, the shared dreams, and the deep love that had blossomed between them. They thanked their family and friends for their endless encouragement, understanding, and presence in their lives.

Emi and Akira also extended their gratitude to the community that had embraced them, the readers who had journeyed with them through their stories, and the world that had offered them endless opportunities for growth, learning, and connection.

As they immersed themselves in gratitude, Emi and Akira felt a profound sense of peace and fulfillment. They understood that gratitude was the key to unlocking joy, resilience, and a deeper connection to life's beauty and abundance.

And so, with hearts full of gratitude, Emi and Akira prepared to embark on the final chapters of their journey, knowing that their story was not just theirs but a shared celebration of love, growth, and the infinite possibilities that awaited them.

LV

Embracing Farewell

As Emi and Akira neared the end of their remarkable journey, they found themselves faced with the inevitable—saying goodbye. It was a bittersweet moment, filled with memories, emotions, and the realization that every ending marked a new beginning.

They embraced farewell with grace, acknowledging the beauty of closure and the opportunity it brought for new adventures, new experiences, and new connections. They thanked each other for the love, support, and shared dreams that had sustained them throughout their journey.

Emi and Akira bid farewell to the characters they had created, the stories they had woven, and the world they had explored through their books. They thanked their readers for joining them on this incredible journey, for sharing their love for stories, and for being a part of their literary adventure.

As they embraced farewell, Emi and Akira felt a sense of gratitude for the journey they had shared, the lessons they had learned, and the love that had enriched their lives. They understood that saying goodbye was not an end but a transition—a stepping stone to new horizons and new chapters waiting to unfold.

And so, with hearts full of gratitude, love, and anticipation for the future, Emi and Akira bid farewell to their 50-book journey of "Love Stories Around the World," knowing that their legacy of love, resilience, and connection would continue to inspire, uplift, and bring joy to the world for generations to come.

LVI

Embracing New Horizons

As Emi and Akira stepped into the dawn of a new chapter, they embraced the excitement of new horizons. They felt a sense of liberation, renewal, and anticipation for the adventures that lay ahead.

They looked back on their journey with gratitude, cherishing the memories, the lessons learned, and the growth that had shaped them into who they were today. They carried the love, resilience, and wisdom gained from their experiences as they embarked on new beginnings.

Emi and Akira embraced the unknown with courage and optimism, knowing that each new horizon brought opportunities for growth, discovery, and transformation. They welcomed the challenges and blessings that awaited them, ready to write new stories, create new memories, and continue their journey of love and fulfillment.

As they embraced new horizons, Emi and Akira felt a deep sense of freedom and possibility. They knew that life was an endless adventure, filled with twists and turns, surprises, and moments of pure joy. They embraced the uncertainty, knowing that every step forward was a step toward new experiences, new connections, and new opportunities to make a difference in the world.

And so, with hearts full of hope, excitement, and gratitude, Emi and Akira embraced the dawn of new horizons, ready to write the next chapter of their lives with love, courage, and a spirit of adventure.

LVII

Embracing Eternal Love

As Emi and Akira reached the final chapter of their journey, they arrived at a profound realization—the essence of their story was eternal love. They understood that love was not bound by time, space, or circumstance, but a timeless force that transcended all barriers.

They embraced the concept of eternal love by recognizing that their journey was a testament to the enduring power of love. Love had guided them through challenges, strengthened their bonds, and filled their lives with meaning, purpose, and joy.

Emi and Akira reflected on the love they had shared—the laughter, the tears, the moments of connection that had woven the fabric of their lives together. They saw love in the beauty of their shared experiences, in the growth they had experienced as individuals and as a couple, and in the legacy of love they had built.

They thanked each other for the love they had given and received, for the support, understanding, and companionship that had sustained them through the highs and lows of life. They expressed gratitude for the journey they had shared, for the lessons learned, and for the profound impact that love had made on their lives.

As they embraced eternal love, Emi and Akira felt a deep sense of peace and fulfillment. They knew that their love story would continue to inspire, uplift, and bring joy to others, for love was a universal language that spoke to the heart and soul of humanity.

And so, with hearts full of gratitude, love, and the promise of eternal connection, Emi and Akira closed the final chapter of their journey, knowing that their love would live on forever, leaving a legacy of love that would echo through time, touching hearts and souls for generations to come.

Farewell To Tokyo: A Love Story Continues

Thank you for joining us on this captivating journey through the streets of Tokyo and the intricacies of Akira and Emi's love story. "Lost Love in Tokyo" marks the second installment in the "Love Stories Around the World" series, a collection of tales that celebrate the universal language of love in diverse cultural settings.

As we bid farewell to Akira and Emi's story, we invite you to continue exploring the myriad facets of love in our upcoming books. Each installment in the series offers a unique perspective, a new set of characters, and a fresh backdrop that will transport you to different corners of the globe.

Stay tuned for our next adventure, where love's journey takes us to yet another captivating destination, filled with passion, intrigue, and the enduring quest for connection.

Until then, may love continue to weave its magic in your lives, inspiring, uplifting, and reminding us all of the timeless power of love to transcend boundaries and touch the soul.

With love and gratitude,

Mikey Katodiya

Author, "Love Stories Around the World" series

Did you love *Lost Love in Tokyo*? Then you should read *First Love in Paris*[1] by Mikey!

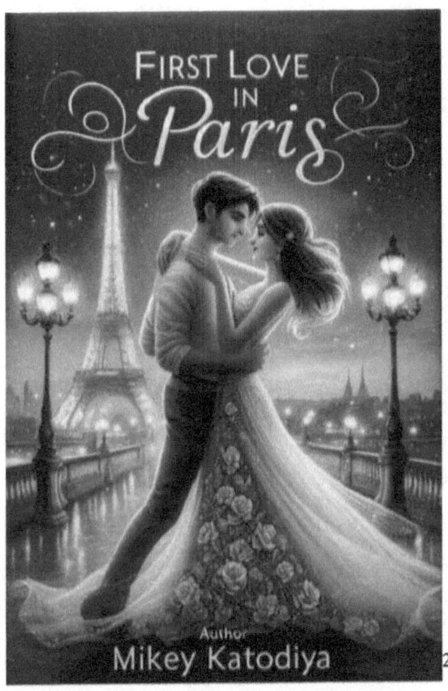

"First Love in Paris" is not just a book; it's a mesmerizing journey that transports readers into the heart of romance, weaving together the intricacies of love, resilience, and the indelible beauty of Parisian charm. From the enchanting streets of Montmartre to the tranquil banks of the Seine, every page of this captivating tale resonates with the timeless essence of first love.

In this literary masterpiece penned by Mikey Katodiya, readers are introduced to Sophie and Alex, two souls destined to find each other amidst the bustling cityscape of Paris. Their love story unfolds like a symphony, with each chapter adding depth and nuance to their passionate connection.

1. https://books2read.com/u/bxM5oq

2. https://books2read.com/u/bxM5oq

The prologue sets the stage, drawing readers into the enchanting world of Paris, where Sophie's vibrant spirit and Alex's steadfast devotion come together in a dance of fate and destiny. As the story progresses, readers are taken on a rollercoaster of emotions, from the exhilarating highs of newfound love to the poignant depths of heartbreak and loss.

Each chapter is a work of art, intricately crafted to immerse readers in the intricacies of Sophie and Alex's relationship. From their first encounter under the twinkling lights of the Eiffel Tower to the tender moments shared in cozy Parisian cafes, every scene is a testament to the power of love to heal, inspire, and transform.

As the story reaches its climax, readers are left breathless by the twists and turns of fate that test Sophie and Alex's bond. Yet, amidst the challenges they face, their love shines brighter than ever, proving that true love is indeed timeless and unbreakable.

The epilogue brings closure to this captivating tale, leaving readers with a sense of fulfillment and longing for more. "First Love in Paris" is not just a book; it's an unforgettable experience that lingers in the mind, reminding us of the enduring power of love and the magic of Parisian romance.

Read more at oximefx@gmail.com.

Also by Mikey

Love Stories Around the World
First Love in Paris
Lost Love in Tokyo

Watch for more at oximefx@gmail.com.

About the Author

Meet, who often goes by the pen name "Mikey," is a passionate writer who believes in the power of storytelling to inspire and heal. Writing has been his creative outlet, allowing him to explore complex emotions and share them with others. 'Yesterday's Love Story' is his debut work, born frompersonal experiences and a desire to connect with readers on a deeply emotional level. Meet hopes his words, written under the pen nameMikey, will resonate with those seeking solace and strength in the face of adversity.

Read more at https://www.instagram.com/bigpicstory.

www.ingramcontent.com/pod-product-compliance
Lightning Source LLC
Chambersburg PA
CBHW031418150726
47989CB00002B/704